Jimmy's Boa Bounces Back

Jimmy's

Boa Bounces Back

TRINKA HAKES NOBLE

pictures by STEVEN KELLOGG

Dial Books for Young Readers

E. P. DUTTON, INC. New York

For Eva C., Erica, and Jessica
T. H. N.

For Lucy the Great
S. K.

Published by Dial Books for Young Readers
A Division of E. P. Dutton, Inc.
2 Park Avenue
New York, New York 10016

Published in Canada by Fitzhenry & Whiteside Limited, Toronto

Library of Congress Cataloging in Publication Data
Noble, Trinka Hakes.
Jimmy's boa bounces back.
Summary: A pet boa constrictor wreaks havoc on a posh garden party.
[1. Boa constrictor—Fiction. 2. Snakes as pets—Fiction.]
I. Kellogg, Steven, ill. II. Title.
PZ7.N6715Ji 1984   [E]   83-14289
ISBN 0-8037-0049-0   ISBN 0-8037-0050-4 (lib. bdg.)

Printed in the U.S.A.
First Edition
(COBE)
10 9 8 7 6 5 4 3 2 1

The full-color artwork was prepared using ink and pencil line
and watercolor washes. It was then camera-separated and reproduced
as red, blue, yellow, and black halftones.

"Hi, Meggie. Where have you been all afternoon?"

"Oh, I had to serve cookies at my mom's garden club meeting,
and you'll never guess who was there."

"Who?"
"Your boa."

"My boa!"

"Yeah, he must have run away from the farm."

"But how did he get to your mom's garden club?"
"Well, actually, my mom wore him."
"She wore him?"
"Yeah, she thought he would spruce up her old gray suit.
  All the garden club ladies thought she looked terrific."

"Wow, my mom wouldn't even touch him!"

"Well…you see…your boa had spent a cold night in the tree outside my house. So I told my mom that snakes don't move around much when they're cold and tired."

"Did he stay still?"
"He might have…except Mrs. Rosebud's wig flew off."

"She had on a flying wig!"

"Actually, it got caught on an alligator's tooth."

"You mean there were alligators at your mom's garden club?"

"Just one. It was Miss Greenleaf's alligator purse.
When she screamed and jumped up, her alligator purse
got caught on Mrs. Rosebud's wig."

"But why did she jump up?"

"Because Miss Peachtree's poodle sneezed and sprayed
cold punch on her back."

"That's impossible. How can a poodle sneeze punch?"

"I guess some got up his nose. You see, he was swimming in the punch bowl."

"You mean Miss Peachtree let her poodle dive into the punch bowl?"

"Actually, Miss Ivy hit her."

"What! The garden club ladies were socking punches
at each other?"

"No, Jimmy. They were sipping punch. But when Miss Ivy fainted, she hit Miss Peachtree, who dropped her poodle in the punch bowl. Nobody wanted any punch after that."

"But what made Miss Ivy faint?"

"Your boa constrictor."

"My boa? I thought he was asleep on your mom's head."

"Well, he sort of woke up when he smelled Miss Ivy's Yellow-Spotted Bongo plant."

"Her Yellow-Spotted what?"

"Well, Miss Ivy was giving a talk to the garden club about this rare Yellow-Spotted Bongo plant from South America. When she mentioned that its only natural enemy is the boa constrictor, well, your boa gobbled it up…pot and all."

"Oh, I see…so she fainted and hit Miss Peachtree, who
dropped her poodle, who sneezed punch on Miss Greenleaf,
whose alligator purse caught Mrs. Rosebud's wig."

"Yeah, and Mrs. Rosebud kept asking me to close the window because she felt a draft."

"But whatever happened to the poodle in the punch bowl, Meggie?"

"Oh, your boa ate it."

"The poodle?"

"No, Jimmy. He ate the punch bowl and saved the poodle!
The poodle was so grateful that he wouldn't leave
your boa's side."

"Wow! Can I serve cookies at your mom's next garden club meeting?"

"I don't think so. She's not a member anymore."

"Well, can we go back there and get my boa?"
"No, your boa left with Miss Peachtree's poodle.
Maybe they're at her house. Let's go see!"

The residence of
MISS OLGA PEACHTREE
AND HER POODLE

"Good, Peaches, you came home all by yourself."